AND EVERYTHING NICE

KIM MORITSUGU

RAVEN BOOKS
an imprint of
ORCA BOOK PUBLISHERS

Library and Archives Canada Cataloguing in Publication

Moritsugu, Kim, 1954-
And everything nice / Kim Moritsugu.
(Rapid reads)

Issued also in electronic formats.
ISBN 978-1-55469-838-7

I. Title. II. Series: Rapid reads
PS8576.072A64 2011   C813´.54   C2010-908116-1

First published in the United States, 2011
Library of Congress Control Number: 2010942253

Summary: After joining a community choir, Stephanie helps
a new friend recover her personal journal from a blackmailer. (RL 4.6)

Disclaimer: This is a work of fiction. Any resemblance of characters to persons,
living or dead, is purely coincidental.

*Orca Book Publishers is dedicated to preserving the environment and has printed this
book on paper certified by the Forest Stewardship Council.*

Orca Book Publishers gratefully acknowledges the support for its publishing
programs provided by the following agencies: the Government of Canada through
the Canada Book Fund and the Canada Council for the Arts, and the Province of
British Columbia through the BC Arts Council and the Book Publishing Tax Credit.

Design by Teresa Bubela
Cover photography by Getty Images

ORCA BOOK PUBLISHERS   ORCA BOOK PUBLISHERS
PO Box 5626, Stn. B   PO Box 468
Victoria, BC Canada   Custer, WA USA
V8R 6S4   98240-0468

www.orcabook.com
Printed and bound in Canada.

14 13 12 11 • 4 3 2 1

To my fellow choirists

PROLOGUE

One day, a few years ago, I found a wallet in the parking lot of the mall where I worked. It was sitting on the ground, open, right under the driver's door of a BMW. Like it fell from the driver's lap when he got out of the car and he didn't notice.

The wallet bulged with cash. Four hundred dollars' worth. And credit cards, a bank card, a driver's license. Everything.

I picked it up and looked around. Was anyone running back to the car in a panic? Nope. The parking lot was empty of pedestrians. And the spot where I stood was out of sight of the mall's outdoor video cameras. No one would see if I slipped the wallet into my bag and kept walking. Or if I removed the cash and dropped the wallet back on the ground.

I stood there for a minute and considered those options. And others. I could leave the wallet where I found it, money and all. Or I could write a note, stick it under the windshield wiper, and turn the wallet into mall security. But I didn't trust some of the guards who worked there.

In the end, I left a note with my name and my cell number. I took the wallet into work. An hour later, I handed it—contents intact—to a relieved man who matched the picture on the driver's license. As soon as he got it, he pulled out a fifty-dollar bill and gave it to me.

"Thanks for your honesty," he said.

I took the fifty. Who wouldn't?

CHAPTER ONE

My mom, Joanne, heard about the community rock choir from her teacher friend, Wendy. I heard about it from Joanne. So no wonder I wasn't interested. Not that I didn't get along with my mom. I did. I mean, I was twenty-four and working full-time as manager of the Gap store in Fairview Mall. But I still lived with her in the townhouse where I grew up.

Joanne liked my company. I liked not paying rent while I was saving to buy a car. For a fifty-five-year-old mom, she was pretty chill. And I was pretty easygoing.

I always have been. Except for when I was nineteen and dropped out of university after one semester. And refused to ever go back.

We were over that, and things were all good between us. But I didn't want to join a choir that met on Tuesday nights in a church and sang rock music. I didn't even like rock music. I was more into pop and urban, top-40-type tunes.

"There *are* pop tunes on the playlist," Joanne said. This was one night in September after the choir's first practice. She came home, warmed up the Thai food I'd ordered in, sat down to eat it and raved about the fun she'd had. "'I Gotta Feeling' by the Black Eyed Peas, for instance. You like that song, don't you?"

"I liked it when it was current."

"And there's a Pointer Sisters song. Talk about music from my era."

"Who the hell are the Pointer Sisters?"

"And there's something by Journey on the list, and 'Honesty' by Billy Joel. I love that song."

"Billy Joel? Are you kidding me? Next you'll say the choir's singing Elton John."

"How did you know?"

"Look, I'm glad you found something to do that you like. A bunch of people your age singing classic rock just doesn't sound like my scene. At all. No offense."

She sagged in her chair. "Oh, Stephanie."

I hated when she said my name like that. Like I'd disappointed her. "What?"

"You were such a good singer when you were little, such a born performer. I think you'd like the choir."

She also thought that by working in retail, I was throwing away some bright future I could have had. The kind of future university grads have.

"I'm not a good singer," I said. "I never was. You just thought I was good because you're my mom."

"How about if you come to choir practice next week and try it, one time? The choir members aren't all my age. Some are in their twenties and thirties. And Wendy and I are in the soprano section. You wouldn't have to hang out with us, or even talk to us. You'd be an alto or a tenor with your raspy voice."

I picked up my phone from the coffee table and pretended it had vibrated. "I missed a call from Nathan. I should call him back. I'm working twelve to nine tomorrow, so I'm staying at his place tonight."

"Say you'll at least think about the choir. I'll pay the fee if you join."

She had that right.

"I'll think about it. I promise."

"Good. Could you pass me my wallet? It's in my purse, on the floor. I want to give you money for the Thai food."

I fished out the wallet and waited while she picked through the receipts, ticket stubs and dollar bills she had stuffed into it.

She said, "That's weird. I thought I had more cash than this. Did you take some out of here already?"

"How could I have done that? I just handed you the wallet two seconds ago."

"I meant before I went to choir practice."

Was she losing her mind? "I wasn't here before your practice, remember? I got home from work after you left. And ordered the Thai food. As you instructed."

She shook her head. "So you did. I'm sorry, I wasn't thinking. Here." She handed me a ten and a twenty. "I thought I had more cash on me. I must have spent it somewhere."

"I love how your first thought when money is missing is that I took it."

"I said I was sorry." She smiled up at me. "I used to take money from my mother's wallet all the time when I was a teenager— a five here, a few singles there. She never noticed."

"Well, I'm not a teenager. And I guess I'm more trustworthy than you were."

So far I was anyway.

CHAPTER TWO

Nathan was the bar manager at an upscale gourmet restaurant downtown called Sterling. It was the kind of place where rich food snobs spent hundreds of dollars on dinner for two with wine. He got off work at eleven thirty, so I met him at his apartment at midnight. When I saw him on his work nights, we usually stayed up for a few hours after he got home. We'd talk and watch TV while he wound down.

That night we drank some good white wine, left over from the restaurant. And we shared an extra dessert Nathan had brought home, a molten chocolate cake. He told me about a table of bankers who had come to Sterling to celebrate a deal and run up a big tab. They'd had cocktails before dinner, four bottles of wine with, and cognac after. And they'd tipped in cash.

"What about you?" he asked. "How was your day? Did you have any problem customers? Anybody who asked for the manager and tried to start a fight?"

"Someone asked for me, but not to complain. The regional director came by on a store visit and I showed her around. She wanted to know what was selling well, and how the merchandising was working out."

"And?"

"She liked me. She said I was a natural."

"A natural what?"

Good question. I thought at first she meant I was a natural at retail, which Joanne would say was no compliment. But when I asked her to explain, she said

I was a natural speaker—clear, smooth and relaxed. "You should see about doing some Gap training videos," she'd said. "They mostly hire actors, but they like to use real employees if they can find someone who's good on camera. Email me your contact info and I'll pass it on. If you're interested."

I told Nathan this, and that I planned to send her an email the next day. To say sure, I was interested. But I wouldn't hold my breath waiting to hear back.

"That's my Steph." Nathan patted my knee. "Future star of training videos."

Was he making fun of me? Because he'd made me sound a little pathetic.

He said, "You'll be trying out for *American Idol* next."

Wrong. I didn't mind the idea of making a training video as a break from my routine. When I was little, I told everyone I wanted to be on TV. So it would be kind of like that. But I was no entertainer.

And by the way, this story is not about how I joined the choir and became a singing star, in case you were wondering. That's not what happened.

"You sound like Joanne," I said. "She's all enthused about this rock choir she's in. She wants me to come with her next Tuesday night and try it out."

"Is it seniors singing Lou Reed songs and shit? I saw something about that on TV once."

"She claims the choir members aren't that old. And the songs are by artists like Elton John and Billy Joel. And Journey, for god's sake."

"Journey's awesome. Don't knock Journey."

"What, you think I should be in the choir too?"

"Only if you want to. Though what else have you got going on a Tuesday night? It's not like you're taking a course." Nathan took online college courses part-time in business management. So that one day he could open his own bar. As if that would ever happen.

I said, "I do things. I work out, I watch TV, I go clubbing with the girls."

"Exactly. What have you got going on that's *interesting*? Not much on the nights you don't see me."

I fake-swung at him and he ducked. "Yeah, well, I'll think about trying the choir. And thanks for ganging up on me with Joanne about it. Thanks a lot."

He turned on the TV with the remote and put his arm around me. "I'm not ganging up. I'm on your side. I want you to enjoy yourself on the nights I'm working. And I know you've been feeling a bit same-old, same-old lately. So why not change it up? Do something new and exciting?"

"The choir would be new, yeah," I said. "But exciting? I don't think so."

It was like I was asking to be proved wrong.

CHAPTER THREE

Joanne and I drove to the next choir practice together in her car, me at the wheel. On the way, she said, "So you know, the choir is big. A hundred and ten people this season, someone said last week. Everyone from teachers, lawyers and media types to young moms, cab drivers and students."

"Sounds like I'll fit right in."

"Are you being sarcastic?"

"Duh."

"You'll be fine. As long as you're prepared for warm-up exercises at the beginning, when we sing scales. And at the end, everyone stands up, joins hands, forms a huge circle inside the church and sings a circle song. It's corny, but it's nice."

"A circle song? Like in preschool?"

"I said it was corny."

"How about if I drop you off right now and drive away? Fast."

"Oh, Stephanie."

"I'm kidding."

"Well, ha-ha. And that's all I wanted to warn you about."

I said, "Why are there so many people in the choir? What do they get out of it?"

"Some people just love to perform. And some are wannabe rock stars, I suppose. Or failed rock stars."

"But not you. Those aren't your reasons. Are they?"

"No. I get to perform every day for the surly teenagers in my classes at school. And I never wanted to be in a band." She didn't say anything else for a minute. Then, "There's something about making music in a group that's more fulfilling than singing alone can ever be. The whole really is greater than the sum of its parts. If you know what I mean."

I didn't, but I was about to find out.

CHAPTER FOUR

The nave of the church buzzed with the voices of a hundred-plus people talking when I walked in. A middle-aged woman greeted me at the door. She had me fill out a form and a name-tag sticker, and she handed me a file folder full of sheet music. She said, "You're welcome to try us out tonight for free and see what you think. If you like it, you can come back next week and pay the hundred-and-fifty-dollar fee!"

Yeah, yeah.

"Now smile," she said and took my picture with a digital camera. "For the choir list."

I took a seat in the tenor section that started five rows back from the front. Around me, assorted tenors—male and female, older and younger—stood and sat, talking to each other like old friends. A woman with wild, curly gray hair, wearing a long hippie-ish dress, hugged a younger woman in jeans and a flannel shirt. Down the aisle, a skinny guy in his late twenties, wearing a white silk scarf around his neck, was talking to another guy his age. I heard him say something about a musical he'd seen onstage. Or was it a musical he'd been in?

In front of the tenors were four rows of women—the altos. Next to them and across the aisle: more women. They had to be the sopranos. Joanne and Wendy were over there, chatting away.

Behind the sopranos sat about twenty men, mostly gray-haired, who made up the bass section. They weren't talking as much as the women. They weren't hugging either.

Though at least one man laughed way too loudly at something another said.

I checked my phone. The practice was supposed to start at seven thirty. It was seven twenty-six. I took out some lip balm from my bag, applied it and tuned in to a conversation between two women seated behind me.

Woman #1: "There'd better be more singing this time, and less talking. Those announcements last week went on forever."

Woman #2: "I know. That killed me. And I hope that tattooed biker guy doesn't sit near us this time. His singing really threw me off."

Woman #1: "Now, now. Not everyone can be as good a singer as you are."

Woman #2: "I *have* been singing for years."

Woman #1: "And your voice is amazing."

There was a pause, during which Woman #2 might have taken a bow. Then she said, "Hey, isn't that Anna Rai coming in the door? She wasn't here last week, was she?"

Woman #1 said, "Is it her? I'm not sure. Yes! It is. Good spotting. And hey, a celebrity."

The tall woman getting the welcome treatment at the door *was* Anna Rai, a local TV personality. She wasn't superfamous, but most people in the city would recognize her. It helped that she looked the same standing at the front of the church as she did on TV. Her long, shiny dark hair was expertly styled. Her flawless eye makeup made her big green eyes look even bigger. And the clothes she wore were TV-worthy—a fitted jacket, a silk shell, two-hundred-dollar jeans over heels. Accessorized with a statement necklace and a designer handbag.

Woman #2: "Is she still on the six o'clock news?"

"No, she hosts a show called *Noontime* now. I caught it last week when I took a sick day. She does these lifestyle segments called 'And Everything Nice.' The one I saw was about how she had her fabulous friends over to her fabulous house to eat fabulous food."

"Who does she think she is, Martha Stewart?"

"She wishes. She should have called the segments, 'Don't You Just Love Me?' Or 'Aren't I Perfect?'"

"Or, 'I'm Fabulous and You're Not.'" And they both laughed.

Could they have gone more quickly from being glad to see Anna Rai to dissing her? Just because she was trying to do something different. And because she was about ten times better-looking than them, was my guess. I was about to turn around and check them out, when Woman #2 said, "Shush, here she comes."

On her way up the aisle, Anna said hi and waved to a few people. Then she stopped right by me and flashed a wide smile.

"Is that seat taken?" She pointed to the empty pew next to me.

"Nope." I slid down to give her some space. "Come on in."

The two women behind me had gone quiet. No doubt listening to every word and staring. Screw them. I knew how to deal with celebrities. I once had Katie Holmes walk into my store when she was in town making a movie. She had her daughter Suri on her hip. She bought three pairs of socks, and I handled the purchase like a pro. Without drooling on her or sucking up.

I said to Anna, "Hi, I'm Steph. This is my first time here, and I'm already wondering if I've made a big mistake in coming."

She laughed. "Hi, I'm Anna. And I know what you mean. The first time I came to choir,

I wasn't sure either. There are a lot of outsized personalities in the group."

The guy with the white scarf picked that moment to fling one end of it around his neck. "Yeah, I noticed that," I said.

Anna unzipped her bag and took out a pen. Before she closed the bag, I peeked inside at its contents: a leather wallet, a small makeup pouch, a packet of tissues, a softcover black notebook.

"Mind you," she said, "I shouldn't talk about people being dramatic. Seeing as I work in television." From a black canvas bag she'd also brought, she pulled out a binder. It contained her sheet music, organized with color-coded dividers. "But I keep a low profile here—I don't try out for the solos or small groups, for instance."

"There are solos and small groups that people try out for?"

She laughed at the expression on my face. "They're optional, don't worry.

Though you'd be surprised how many people audition. Or maybe you wouldn't."

Someone coughed to my right. A sandy-haired guy around my age, with a buzz cut and an earring, had sat down a foot away. He was studying his music. Or was he trying to hide that he was shy?

"Hey, Brandon," Anna said. "Good to see you back. How are you doing?"

"I'm okay. I'm not too sure about this season's music though. Have you seen the list? That song 'Good Vibrations' is old enough to be my father."

Anna chuckled. "It's a classic, all right. This is Steph, by the way. She's here tonight for the first time."

"Welcome to the tenors," Brandon said. "And to the sixties, apparently."

A few minutes later, Brandon turned away to speak to someone else.

"Being here reminds me of the first day of high school," I said to Anna.

"When everyone breaks off into cliques and starts competing to be the hippest or the baddest."

I thought about the people I worked with at the store, how they formed alliances and complained about each other. And about the kitchen staff at Sterling. Nathan was always telling me about their feuds. "Actually, maybe all life is like high school."

Anna waved and mouthed hi at a heavyset man with a neck tattoo, wearing a *Sticky Fingers* T-shirt. He waved back and turned into the pew behind us.

"I have no desire to go back to high school," she said. "But I do like to people watch in large groups like this. Maybe it's because I'm a journalist. I'm interested in how people behave and interact in social situations. They say everyone has a story, and I'm curious about those stories." She smiled. "Or maybe I'm just nosy."

I imagined the two women behind me exchanging a glance when they heard her say that. They probably thought she was full of shit, or full of herself. All I knew was that *I* didn't have a story. Not yet.

The accompanist played a fanfare on the piano, and everyone around me stood up. "Ready or not, here we go," Anna said. And we got up and started to sing scales.

CHAPTER FIVE

The practice went better than I expected. Meaning that it wasn't totally lame.

The choir director was a middle-aged bald man named Richard. He had a paunch and a sense of humor. His jokes were not as funny as he thought they were, but I liked how he handled the backtalk and questions from the choir members. And there was a lot of backtalk to handle. Imagine a room full of troublemakers of all ages—that was the choir.

In the first half of the practice, we worked on bits of four songs. Richard taught each section its part of a twelve-bar passage, say, while the other sections sat and listened. Once we'd all run through our parts, he rehearsed us together. And guess what? To be part of a group singing a song in four-part harmony *was* kind of cool. Even if a lot of people, including me, weren't hitting the correct notes or rhythms.

I'd thought most of the choir members would be good singers, but the quality of the voices around me was mixed. Anna sang quietly—I could hardly hear her. Brandon, who reeked of cigarette smoke, asked me twice what bar we were on in the sheet music. The *Sticky Fingers* man yelped like Mick Jagger when we sang some of "You Can't Always Get What You Want." And behind me, Ms. All That sang loudly, in a show-offy way. Like she was singing opera. Plus, she always sang the melody, even when the tenor part was backup or harmony.

An hour in, Richard made some announcements. First, that members weren't only expected to attend weekly practices. There would also be separate practices for each section. All leading up to the concert in December.

It sounded like a big time commitment. If I stayed.

Richard said, "Lastly, I've got the sign-up sheets here for the small groups and solo parts. I'll leave them on the piano. If you want to try out, sign up during the break. Auditions will be held in a few weeks' time. Now, let's take fifteen minutes."

Anna said, "I'm going to try to beat the line to the washroom." And took off. Almost everyone else scattered. A bunch mobbed the piano and the sign-up sheets. A group of smokers headed outside, cigarette packs in hand. Several women

Joanne's age, including Joanne, trooped off to the washroom.

I didn't need to pee and I didn't smoke, so I stayed sitting. I turned on my phone and texted Nathan a report:

```
I'm at choir practice. It's not
bad so far. I know. I can't believe
it either. Most of the people here
are nuts though. In a funny way.
   XO
```

I checked my emails and my Facebook news feed. I stood up, stretched, looked around the church. The pew behind me was empty—no sign of the two chatty women, or of Sticky Fingers. I saw Anna though, almost hidden, in a back corner of the nave. She was sitting on a wooden chair with a high back, like a throne. She seemed to be writing in a notebook.

Brandon was working his way down the pew behind me, sliding on his ass toward the center aisle. "Are you changing rows?" I said. Trying to be friendly.

"What?" He looked blank. "Wasn't I sitting in this row?"

I shook my head. "No, you were up here, with me. But I won't be insulted if you switch."

"No," he said. "I'm just confused. I'll be back. I have to go do something first." And he slithered down the pew and scooted to the back of the church.

Sticky Fingers lumbered over and sat down. Followed by the two women from before. Woman #2 entered talking. "So how pregnant are you?"

A female voice I hadn't heard before said, "Six months. But I'm huge. Don't ask how much weight I've gained."

Woman #1: "I've seen bigger at that stage."

Pregnant said, "I've got three months to go and I'm already losing my mind.

I can't sleep. I can't concentrate at work. And I could have sworn I had a hundred bucks in my wallet earlier today. Now I only count eighty."

Woman #2: "I try not to carry cash. The less I have on me, the less I spend."

Pregnant said, "I only had that much because I've been collecting at my office for a wedding gift for my boss. But I was sure I'd collected a hundred bucks."

Woman #1: "Maybe you used the gift money to buy lunch. Consider it your commission."

Woman #2: "Yeah! Why should you shop for the office for free?"

"Good point," Pregnant said. "Oh hell. I have to go pee. Again."

When I heard her get up and go, I half turned in my seat. And pretended I wasn't totally scoping out the two women. They were about the same age as Anna— mid-thirties, I'd say. They weren't as good-looking as her, but they weren't ugly. Especially now that they were smiling. At me. Woman #1 said, "Hi, I'm Carmen, and this is Kristi."

"Hi, I'm Steph." I pointed to my name tag.

Kristi said, "I heard you say before that you're new to the choir this season. We are too. What do you think of it so far?"

"I like it more than I thought I would. I've never sung in a choir before. Have you?"

Carmen had sung in choirs and other groups before, for sure. And she'd done years of vocal training. She'd found out about this choir when she and Kristi became friends with Pauline, the tenor section head. She'd urged them to join, and now here they were.

Carmen said, "So that was Anna Rai sitting next to you, right?"

"Yup."

"What's she like?"

"She seems nice. The same as she seems on TV."

Kristi said, "We were talking before about that *Noontime* show she's on. She does these bits on food and decorating and home stuff. Have you seen those?"

"No."

Carmen said, "In the segment I saw, she hosted a champagne brunch at her house. That's some swanky house she's got."

Kristi said, "Must be nice to get paid the big bucks for being born pretty. Though there's something mannish about her jaw, have you noticed? I'd get that fixed if I were her."

Carmen leaned forward. "The dumbest part was when she pretended to make a six-layer coconut cake, then pretended to eat it. She took one bite and made, like, sex noises. When everyone knows there's no way she eats cake in real life. Have you seen how skinny she is? Her arms and legs are like sticks."

Kristi: "She must have spit out the cake off camera."

Carmen: "Those shows are so fake. They probably hire actors to be her friends. And the house is a set. You have to wonder who she slept with to get that gig."

I didn't know what to say. I had no reason to protect or defend Anna, but I didn't want to tear her apart either. Not like those two piranhas.

When the pianist played the fanfare again, I saw Anna get up and come toward us.

I turned around and faced the altar. "No wonder she goes off by herself during the break," I said.

Carmen said, "What was that?"

But Richard was talking about the next song to work on, and Anna and Brandon had slipped back into the pew, so I didn't have to answer. Didn't want to either.

CHAPTER SIX

Nathan didn't get why I decided to join the choir. When I told him about my first night at practice, he said, "It sounds like everyone bugged you. So why go back?"

"Not everyone bugged me. Anna Rai was nice. This guy Brandon was okay. And Richard, the choirmaster, is kind of funny."

"Isn't it like being at work, though? Having to deal with people's egos and listen to their bitching? I thought you got enough of that at the store."

"It's different at choir. I'm not the boss, so I can do whatever I want. And watching these people act out is like watching a soap." I swung my leg over his on the couch. "Maybe it's because I work in customer service, but I like seeing how people behave and interact in social situations. I'm curious that way."

Was I, really? Or did I just like how Anna's words sounded coming out of my mouth? I wasn't sure.

"Don't get me wrong," Nathan said. "If you like it, do it. But if the girl who sat behind you and sang too loud makes you crazy, don't."

That's what was weird. Kristi and Carmen and the dudes with attitude *had* made me crazy. But in a way that made me want to go back for more.

* * *

At the second practice, Anna and I sat in the same pew as before, in front of Kristi and Carmen. The way high school kids pick a seat on the first day of class and stick with it the whole year.

After we'd taken out our music and stowed our bags, Kristi and Carmen said hi to me and introduced themselves in a friendly way to Anna. You'd never know they'd put her down, big-time, behind her back the week before.

Anna said, "Are you two going to try out for the small groups and solos?"

Kristi said, "Carmen will. She has an amazing voice. She'll get some solos, for sure."

Carmen said, "Nothing's for sure, Kristi. There are a lot of factors that go into casting decisions."

Casting decisions? What did Carmen think she would be trying out for?

Carmen said, "I bet the best parts go to the veterans. Isn't that how everything in life works? It's all about who you know and who your connections are. When it should be about talent. Right, Anna?"

Anna deflected Carmen's comment with a smile. She said, "Brandon would know more about the selection process than me. He sang in a small group at the last concert. Didn't you, Brandon?"

Brandon had slid into our pew from the other end. Anna was in the middle between us, but I could still smell the tobacco smoke on him. He said, "Yeah, I was in the all-guy group that sang 'Confessions' last season." He indicated Sticky Fingers, who was sitting in the pew in front of us this time. "Oscar was in the group too."

"You guys were good!" Anna said.

I said, "'Confessions'? The Usher song?"

Sticky Fingers turned around, and I got a good view of the huge snake tattoo on his neck. "Yeah." He let loose a wheezy laugh. "Me, Brandon and a couple of rich lawyers from the bass section sang it.

I was the only dude in the group who was a believable thug, but hey. We gave it our all. Right, Brandon?"

Brandon said, "We sure did." And he winked at me behind Oscar's back. As if to say, *Can you believe I sang in a group with this lowlife?*

At the break that night, Kristi and Carmen started more introductions among the tenors. Within a few minutes, I'd met twenty people. I knew I wouldn't remember all their names, so I gave them nicknames. Among the women: Green Hair, Freckles, Pregnant and Old Hippie. Some of the men: Tall Guy, Pointy Shoes, Kramer and Ponytail.

Two practices and weeks later, I still didn't know all their names. But I knew their faces and their voices. I'd also gotten to know Anna better. And become curious enough about her to set the PVR at home to record her show.

Joanne walked into the room one night when I was fast-forwarding through a *Noontime* episode. As soon as the "And Everything Nice" segment title came up on the screen, she said, "Wait. Is this based on that old sexist poem? 'Sugar and spice and everything nice, that's what little girls are made of'?"

"Seems to be."

"Let's see it."

The opening shot showed Anna sitting at an antique desk in a sunny living room. The camera zoomed in on her hand, writing in a notebook that looked like the one she'd had at choir practice.

The camera panned up to her face. She said, "Some people consider it old-fashioned to write in longhand, with a pen, on paper. But I love to record my thoughts about what I've seen and heard and read each day."

Joanne said, "Hey, I like that. A plug for journal-keeping. Go literacy!"

Anna's voiceover continued over a montage of images. "Recording my impressions of people and places is like writing a book of memories." She taped a maple leaf into her journal. She made an I've-got-an-idea face and wrote something down. Her hand added the last two words to the sentence: *I love the brilliant colors and cool breezes of fall.*

Joanne said, "Could she be more trite?"

"What does trite mean, again?"

"Banal, hackneyed. Lame."

We were back to a shot of Anna sitting, facing the camera. "The act of writing helps me remember what I've done," she said. "And what I want to do." She closed the notebook. "And today, I want to go to a local farmers' market and buy some root vegetables!"

"That notebook she has?" Joanne said. "It's a fancy French brand that aspiring writers use. Hemingway used them."

"Why do you even know that?"

"How often do I have to tell you? English teachers know everything."

On screen, Anna stood in front of a market table. She held a squash in her hand and talked to a farmer.

"This is boring," I said.

"Do you think she'll cook that squash with sugar and spice?" Joanne said. "Because that would be 'nice.' Five bucks says she does."

"No bet. She will do that, for sure. Niceness is her thing. Her niche."

"Poor her then," Joanne said and went upstairs to prepare her classes.

CHAPTER SEVEN

The following Monday, I got an email from a guy named Andrew, the assistant to the regional director. It said:

Hi Stephanie:

The RD asked me to contact you about your interest in training videos. I've checked with the training department and they'd like to see some footage. Could you put together a 5-minute video of yourself walking and talking in close-ups and long shots and email it to me for

*passing on? You could shoot it at your
store before opening one day.*
  Thanks!
  Andrew

That night Nathan was off work, so
he came over for a pasta dinner cooked by
Joanne. Once we'd sat down, I told them
about the email.

"So they want me to make a video,"
I said. "Like an audition."

Joanne served some pasta into a dish and
passed it to me. "That's great, Steph! Maybe
the job isn't such a dead end after all. But
why didn't you tell me about this training
video idea earlier? When it first came up?"

I inhaled the scents of lemon and
chicken coming off the plate and passed it
to Nathan. "Because I knew you'd be overly
interested and ask too many questions."

Nathan said, "Be nice, Steph."

Joanne said, "Okay, here's a question: Where are you supposed to get a video camera?"

"I know a guy who has a camera I could borrow," Nathan said. "I could do the filming. And edit it on my computer. I took a film course once and learned how."

Joanne gave me my dish. "It doesn't seem right that you have to make the video yourself. When it was the boss's idea that you try out."

"That's how jobs are these days, Joanne," Nathan said. "You want something, you have to go after it. Make it happen."

"These days?" Joanne said.

"Sorry, but it's true. Times have changed since you were young. This is great pasta, by the way. I'm loving the rapini in it. And the pine nuts."

"I'm glad you like it. And thanks for pointing out I'm not young anymore."

She smiled to show that she wasn't really pissed off and turned to me. "You know what you could do? Make it like a music video. Sing as you walk through the store." To the tune of "Good Vibrations," she sang, "Tee, Tee, Tee-ee, Tee-shirts and jee-eans."

Nathan laughed. I didn't. "I won't sing. I'll talk," I said. "I'll say what I say when I train new staff. I'm not going to make a big production out of it. If they like what they see, good. If they don't, they don't."

Nathan took out his phone. "So when do you want to do this? I should text my guy about the camera."

"How about Wednesday morning before opening? We'd have to get there early though, like at eight thirty."

He started texting. "I can do early. If you buy me an extra-large coffee on the way in."

"What about hair and makeup and wardrobe?" Joanne said. "Who's going to do that?"

"I will." I already knew what I'd wear—some new work-type clothes that had come into the store that day. Something grown-up.

"I wish I could help," Joanne said. "You can't shoot the video on a weekend day when I'm available?"

"We'll be better off without you, Mom. You know what they say about too many cooks." Nathan kicked me under the table, so I said, "Thanks for the offer though."

"Okay, but Nathan, be sure to shoot Steph from flattering angles. Make her look good."

"That'll be easy. Steph always looks good."

"Aren't you the charmer tonight," she said. "Would you like more pasta?"

CHAPTER EIGHT

I came to the next night's choir practice straight from work. I was early and the door to the church nave was closed. A sign posted on it said:

SILENCE PLEASE. SMALL GROUP
AUDITIONS IN PROGRESS.
ENTER QUIETLY
OR COME BACK AT 7:25!

I needed a coffee anyway. I'd had a long day. I'd had to fire a sales associate after he showed up half an hour late, for the fifth time. Then I had to fill in for him at the register after he left. And that afternoon

I'd caught a shoplifter, a punky girl about twenty.

I'd seen her before, lurking around in a sweatshirt, dirty jeans and Converse sneakers. This time I was ringing up a sale when I spotted her across the floor, standing behind a table display of Henley shirts. She had her back to me, but I saw her slip two shirts into a shopping bag she carried. I got someone to finish my sale, and I snuck up on her. When I asked if she'd like to try on those shirts, she dropped the bag and ran away fast. Which was lucky. I would have had to call the cops on her if she hadn't.

I hated calling the cops. An arrest always caused a scene in the store, in front of the paying customers. And going to court to testify was such a hassle. The hearing doesn't take place for months, and when you go to the courthouse, you wait for hours for the case to be called. Then you see the shoplifter waiting too. With a legal-aid lawyer and maybe a parent or an older sibling who looks upset. And the cops sit around joking with each other like they don't give a shit, which they don't. And the judge sometimes yells at the thief, to try to scare them straight or whatever. You end up feeling sad and sorry for the person you collared. Rather than feeling that justice is being done. I did anyway.

There was a coffee shop a block away from the church. With twenty-five minutes to kill before the practice started, I walked over to it, ordered a large coffee and looked around for a seat.

The shop was crowded, mostly with people I didn't think were choir members. Except for Anna, over in the corner. She was sitting at a high counter with a coffee cup beside her, writing.

I wasn't going to disturb her, but she saw me and waved me over. "Hi, Steph! There's space here. Come sit."

I set my coffee down and motioned to the notebook in front of her. "Is that the journal you used on *Noontime*?"

"It's the same kind. I go through a new notebook every few months."

"My mom's big on journals. And writing. But when I had to keep a journal in high school for English class, I hated doing it. What I wrote was so boring."

"You don't feel a need to express yourself then?"

"I guess not. I don't get why people have blogs either. Or go on Twitter. Like their lives are so interesting."

She said, "I have to blog and tweet for my work; it's part of my job. But my journal is just for me. It really helps me sort out what I'm doing and feeling. And it's cheaper than going to a shrink." She slipped the notebook into her bag. "But are you saying you saw one of my 'And Everything Nice' segments on *Noontime*?"

I didn't want to seem like a stalker. I said, "I caught it this week, randomly. The farmers' market one."

"What did you think of it?"

"It was, uh, nice."

"You liked it that much, huh?"

"I don't think I'm in the target market. I hardly ever watch daytime TV. But the root-vegetable mash that you made with the maple syrup? It looked good. My mother said she would make it sometime soon." Okay, she might have said that if she'd watched more of the show.

"But you wouldn't?"

"I don't cook much."

"Neither do most people your age, I'm thinking." She lowered her voice. "I'm also one of the producers of *Noontime*, and between you and me, we're working on getting national distribution. So it should appeal to as wide an audience as possible. Including people like you. Tell me: Do you watch *any* food or lifestyle shows on TV?"

"Some. My boyfriend works at Sterling, a restaurant downtown. He's the bar manager."

"I've been to Sterling. The food is excellent."

"So sometimes we watch the shows about restaurant kitchens. The ones with yelling and swearing are entertaining."

"Hmm. Then there's me, being boring and nice."

"Don't forget about the sugar and spice."

Her face lit up. "You know, that's a good idea. I *should* make the segments spicier. More edgy. To appeal to a younger audience. And to men. Let me make a note of that." She took out her notebook, wrote the word *SPICIER* on a blank page and closed it again. Put it away. "So, how are you enjoying the choir these days?"

"I like it. Partly because of what you said. It *is* interesting to watch people in action."

"Especially when so many are creative people."

"That's one way to describe them," I said, and she laughed.

On the way back to the church, she asked about my job.

"Do you see yourself staying there and climbing the corporate ladder?" she said. "Or are you putting in time while you pursue something more artistic?"

I would have snapped at Joanne if she asked me those same questions, laughed at the artistic part and told her to back off. But I liked Anna showing interest in me.

"I can see moving up," I said. "I might transfer to head office. Get involved with making training videos." I shouldn't have said that, I know. Shouldn't have talked about something that probably wouldn't happen.

I guess I wanted to come off like someone with a plan and a clue. Someone like her.

She said, "Training videos? What are they like?"

So I told her about the RD and the email from her assistant. And that Nathan and I were making a video the next morning at the store. And she looked totally interested in what I was saying. As if she were interviewing me on her show. She said, "I can see what the senior person saw in you. You have an appealing manner. You're engaging. Have you done on-camera work before?"

"No. Never."

"Oh."

"Have you got any tips on how we should shoot the video?" What the hell. There was no harm in asking, right?

She did. For the next few minutes, she gave me a crash course on how to act on TV. She talked about what to wear and what not to wear. About makeup and lipstick colors.

About making eye contact with the camera, and how to look expressive. She told me to memorize and rehearse my lines before-hand. And to decide in advance which words in each sentence should be stressed.

We stopped outside the church, and she quickly demonstrated the most flattering ways to stand, walk and angle my face and body toward the camera.

"Thank you so much," I said when she'd wrapped up. "I hope I can remember every-thing you've said when we do the taping tomorrow."

"I could email you a checklist," she said. "I wrote one up a while back when I visited a high school class for a Career Day. Your email address is on the choir list, right? I'll send it to you when I get home tonight."

"That would be great."

She opened the church door and held it open for me. "Here we go," she said. "Into the breach." And I laughed like I got the joke.

CHAPTER NINE

At the break that night, Anna went off to make a phone call. I wandered over to the soprano section and said hi to Joanne and Wendy. They invited me to come out for a drink at a nearby pub with some choir people after practice. I said no thanks without saying, "God, no." And Joanne and I arranged that I'd drive the car home.

I put on my jacket and went outside. On the church steps, I ran into Sticky Fingers on his way back in. He said, "Damn right," to someone behind him, then laughed his dirty-sounding laugh. I turned up my collar and kept going. I wouldn't want to meet him in the mall parking lot late at night. Or in the alley behind the church.

I walked down to the traffic light, crossed the street and bought an iced tea at a convenience store. When I came back inside the church a few minutes later, Kramer and Old Hippie were both bent over in our pew, looking for something on the floor. Anna stood in the aisle, wringing her hands. Her face was flushed. Other tenors were grouped in a semi-circle around our pew. Like at a funeral.

I walked up to Kristi, who was on the outside edge of the group. Not next to Carmen, for once. "What's going on?" I said.

"Anna lost her notebook." She put her hand to her mouth in mock concern. "Time to call for a search party."

The pianist played the fanfare, and everyone began to move back into the seats.

Including Kristi, who rolled her eyes at me as she went.

"Thanks for looking," Anna said to Kramer and Old Hippie. "I'm sure it will turn up somewhere." The worry lines between her eyebrows said otherwise.

I sat down. Richard started talking about the dynamics in the next song. I whispered to Anna, "Are you okay? Is anything else missing?"

"No. Just my journal. I don't know where it could be. I didn't leave it at the coffee shop, did I?"

"No, you put it in your bag. I saw you."

"Yes, of course I did. But where is it now? What could have happened to it?"

From behind his lectern, Richard said, "When I talk about a crescendo here, I mean that the volume should slowly increase when you sing this passage. I DO NOT MEAN THAT THE VOLUME OF YOUR TALKING RIGHT NOW SHOULD BE AUDIBLE."

Shit. He was looking right at Anna and me.

Someone laughed nervously, and Freckles turned around and gave us an evil stare to go with Richard's. Screw them all. On the edge of my music sheet, I wrote: *We'll talk about this later*. I showed it to Anna. She bit her lip and nodded.

Just before practice ended, Anna rushed up to the front of the church and made an announcement. She described the notebook, said she'd lost it and asked anyone who found it to please, please let her know. Behind me, Kristi muttered to Carmen, "All this fuss for a notebook. What a drama queen."

After we'd all joined hands and sung the circle song, Anna and I left the church together and stood outside on the sidewalk. "Let's mentally retrace your steps," I said. "As best as you can remember."

She'd made her phone call, come back to our pew and sat down. She took out the notebook and made a note of a tricky passage in a song that she wanted to review later at home. Then she put the notebook away in her bag, which was on the floor at her feet. For five minutes or so, she walked around and talked to some tenors. Freckles, whose real name was Pauline, was the section leader. When she'd said that the first sectional practice would be held on Saturday afternoon, Anna had looked in her bag for her journal to write down the date. Only the journal wasn't there.

I said, "There's a sectional practice this Saturday?"

"At one o'clock. Pauline said she'd email everybody the details. But what am I going to do? I want my journal back. I need it."

"Because your notes are important to you. I understand. Your ideas for your new show must be, like, trade secrets."

She shook her head. "That's not the only reason."

"You're upset because those notebooks are expensive?"

"No. Though they are costly. No, the problem is that I've written some personal things in the journal, private things."

Oh. "You don't have to answer this, but what kind of private things?"

She hesitated. "Things I wouldn't want anyone to read. It's hard to explain."

"I'm sorry. I don't want to pry."

"You're not prying. You're being a good friend. I'm going back in to look again. Maybe it got kicked under another pew. Or tucked in with the hymn books on a shelf."

I offered to go in with her and help her search. She said no. She'd taken up enough of my time. I should go home. She'd email me if she found it.

"Thanks for listening," she said. "I know I'm making too big a deal out of this. And after I told you I was low-profile compared to the other choir people! Forgive me."

I said there was nothing to forgive, and goodnight, and I let her be.

And for all the TV crime shows I'd watched in my time, I'm sorry to say that thoughts of blackmail didn't even cross my mind. They crossed hers though.

CHAPTER TEN

Anna emailed me later that night. She said:

Hi Steph:

I searched all over the church and didn't find the notebook :(

As promised, I've attached the on-camera checklist.

Good luck with the filming.

Anna

I printed off her checklist, read it over and spent an hour rehearsing my script in front of the mirror. I laid out my clothes for the next morning, and at eleven o'clock, before Joanne even got home from her post-practice drinks, I went to bed. I wanted to look rested when I woke up.

To be honest, in the time between practice and going to sleep, I didn't think much about Anna's journal. If someone in the choir had found it, they would have told her by now. And if a random stranger found it, they'd probably throw it away. So what if her notes went into the garbage? How important could things like the word *spicier* written on a page be?

The next day, Joanne and I were up and getting ready for work at the same time.

"You look beautiful," she said when I came out of my room, hair and makeup done. "Like a TV star."

"Mo-om," I said and rolled my eyes.

"My bad. I forgot I'm not supposed to act proud of you. Ever. Do you want a lift to the mall? I have enough time to make the detour on the way to school."

In the car, I asked how the pub night had gone.

"It was fun. About fifteen people from the choir came, men and women both. A group of them go out for drinks after every practice."

"Did you meet any cute guys?"

She shot me an Are-you-kidding? look. "No. But the conversation was lively. The first topic of the night was your friend Anna Rai. That was weird, wasn't it? That tearful announcement she made about the missing notebook?"

"Yeah. I talked to her about it a bit afterward. It was her private journal that was lost. She doesn't want anyone reading it."

She chuckled. "Wendy was making Nancy Drew jokes. She kept referring to it as *The Mystery of the Missing Notebook*."

I didn't say anything.

She said, "Nancy Drew? The teenage detective?"

"Wasn't that a movie a few years ago?"

"I was talking about the Nancy Drew books. As you know. Anyway, a man at the table who's a psychologist said the oddest thing about the incident was that Anna looked guilty when she stood up in front of the choir. As if she'd done something wrong."

"Yeah? What does he know?"

"Probably nothing. I'm just telling you what I heard. They sure like to gossip, that crew."

"God, the choir really *is* like high school."

Joanne took that as a cue to start singing "High School Musical," one tune that was *not* on the choir's playlist. And that was the end of that conversation.

CHAPTER ELEVEN

Nathan was sitting on a bench in front of the Gap store, pretending to be asleep, when I came down the hall. The only other people in sight were elderly mall walkers. I handed him a large coffee and the shot list I'd prepared. "Read this while you drink your coffee."

He peered at the list with one eye open. "You made a shot list?"

"Yup." I unlocked the main door, turned off the alarm and let Nathan in. When I'd turned on the lights, I said, "I'll hang up my jacket. Then I'll be ready to go. How do I look?"

"You look gorgeous, gorgeous." He pulled out a small video camera and a folded-up tripod from the bag he carried. "I'll get set up."

My shot list was basic: shot #1 was of my head and shoulders while I introduced myself. Shot #2 was of me demonstrating how to fold T-shirts—yes, there is a proper way. And in shot #3 I gave a tour of the women's section of the store. Pretty simple. Though it took us over an hour to shoot those three things from different angles. To end up with twenty-five minutes of video that Nathan would edit down to five.

None of the staff would show up until 9:50 AM, but I made sure Nathan was packed and ready to go by 9:35. The less anyone at work knew about any aspirations I might have, the better.

On his way out, Nathan stopped on the men's side of the store, picked up a sweater from the top of a pile and stroked it. "I like this," he said.

"I'll remember that on your birthday. Now go. And thanks for being my cameraman."

He looked at the ceiling. "What's to stop me from slipping out with this under my arm? Have you got video security in here?"

"We sure do. And I have to check your bag before you go."

"Are you kidding?"

"I'm not. It's procedure. So put down the sweater, show me there's nothing in your bag except the camera and tripod, and say goodbye."

"My babe, the responsible boss. I love it." He put down the sweater and opened his bag wide for me. "Do I get an all-clear?"

"Yes. Thanks again. I'll see you tonight."

I locked the door after him, went into the back room and turned on my phone. I had three messages. One was a text from Joanne:

How'd the shoot go? Bet you were swell! Love you.

The second was from one of the sales associates, asking what time her shift started. I texted her back and checked the third message. It was an email, from Anna. It said:

Steph:

Are you working today? Can we meet briefly to talk? Wherever you like. Please let me know. It's important.

Anna

What the hell? I sent a reply, saying I was at the store and couldn't take a real break till two, when the assistant manager came in.

Her message came back right away. She'd meet me outside the store at two fifteen. She'd be wearing a scarf and sunglasses.

A scarf and sunglasses, for god's sake. A getup right out of Nancy Drew.

CHAPTER TWELVE

Anna spilled the beans as soon as we sat down on a bench outside the mall, far from the foot traffic. "I'm sorry to burden you with my problems, but I don't know who else to tell, who else I can trust."

What made her think she could trust me? I mean, she could. But how did she know that, after meeting me only a month before? I said, "Don't be sorry. What happened?"

"Swear you won't breathe a word of this to anyone."

I felt stupid, but I said, "I swear."

"Someone got in touch about the journal. He wants ten thousand dollars for it, or he'll send it to *The Star*."

"Who got in touch? How, and when?"

She pulled her scarf—a fancy silk one—down lower on her forehead, which made her look like she was in disguise. Or was a nutjob. And she told me the latest developments in what I couldn't help thinking of as *The Mystery of the Missing Notebook*.

She'd received an email that morning from someone called nobody123@gmail.com. She showed it to me on her phone. It said:

I have your notebook. It will cost you $10,000 to get it back. Considering the incriminating shit you wrote in the book, $10,000 is a bargain and you know it. If you want it back, tell NO ONE about this message and bring an envelope containing the cash to the sectional this Saturday.

I'll give you instructions later on how to make the drop. If you don't answer this email by tomorrow, and don't pay up, I'll send the notebook to The Star. You know what that would mean. Goodbye to two careers: yours and a certain someone else's.

There was no signature.

I said, "Are you sure this is for real? Could it be someone's idea of a prank?"

"No. He knows what I wrote—things that could get me into trouble."

"And can you tell me what those things are yet, or not?"

Her eyes got wet. "No."

"Okay then," I said. "Why are you referring to the blackmailer as 'he,' by the way? What makes you think a guy sent this?"

She looked thoughtful. That is, the small part of her face that wasn't covered by the scarf and sunglasses looked thoughtful.

"I just assumed," she said. "But it could be a woman."

I could already think of two female tenors who weren't Anna's biggest fans. Could their resentment of her success and status have led them to blackmail?

"Did you check the choir email list for this email address?"

"Yes. It wasn't there."

I said, "So the blackmailer isn't a total idiot."

She covered her face with her hands and mumbled through them. "I don't know what to do. I'm such a mess. I don't even know what I'm doing here, talking to you about this when he—or she—said to tell no one. Someone could be watching us right now!"

Jesus. No one was watching us. "Why *are* you telling me?"

"Because you were sympathetic about it last night. Unlike those two bitches who sit behind us. Do they think I don't see them making fun of me whenever I open my mouth?"

She was dead serious, but I laughed. "Kristi and Carmen *are* bitchy."

"I'm telling you because I can't tell anyone I work with, or any of my friends who have media jobs. And you seem street-smart. I thought you might know what to do."

Is that what I was? Book-dumb and street-smart? I could run with that, try it on for size.

"Let's review what we know and don't know," I said.

The blackmailer was a tenor in the choir, male or female. Anna had no idea who it could be. And clearly the perp wanted to keep it that way.

"Maybe we could trace where the email was sent from?" she said. "I could ask one of the IT guys at work to look into it, make up a fake reason why."

78

"I wouldn't bother. The IT guy might get suspicious. And the blackmailer probably created and accesses the email account on a public computer. At a library or an internet café. Somewhere that doesn't track its users."

We knew that the blackmailer had been at the last practice and would attend the sectional one. And that he or she had read the journal and recognized that its contents could wreck Anna's career if they were made public.

I said, "The big question right now is this: Are you willing to pay ten thousand dollars to get the journal back?"

"No. Yes. I don't know!"

I had fifteen minutes left on my lunch break. "There's not much I can do to help until you decide."

She took a deep, shaky breath. "Okay, yes. I totally don't want to and I hate that I've been put in this awful corner where I have to consider it. But yes, I'll pay."

"Can you come up with ten thousand in cash by Saturday?"

In a small voice, she said, "Yes."

"So do you want to pay up and get your journal back? Or do you want to try and foil the blackmailer, and catch him or her in the act?"

For the first time that day, I saw the trace of a smile on her face. "How about if we get the journal back *and* foil the blackmailer?"

Who's we? I wanted to say. But I'd already started to think of a plan.

CHAPTER THIRTEEN

In the time that remained in my break, Anna and I composed this reply for her to send to nobody123:

Got your message. I want my journal back. I'll pay to get it if I have to.

She wanted to add in some emotional stuff. Talk about how being blackmailed made her feel betrayed and exposed. Say what it was like to have her privacy invaded. I told her not to. No point in giving the blackmailer any more material.

After she'd sent the email from her phone and sworn me to secrecy *again*, we agreed to meet at her house at eight that evening. Then we went our separate ways. She drove back to the TV studio, and I returned to the store. Where my day went by fast, for once. I spent the slow parts thinking about how to catch the blackmailer.

I got off work at six, went home and had dinner with Joanne. And told her I was going out after for a few drinks with my friend Jenn. To make up for that little lie, I gave her a full account of the filming Nathan and I had done that morning. I even stood up and acted out the T-shirt-folding sequence.

At eight o'clock, I knocked on Anna's back door—her idea. In case anyone was watching the front one. She let me in, offered me a glass of wine and showed me into a living room straight out of an interior-design-magazine spread. It was all beige and cream and black, with teal accents.

She said, "I still haven't heard back from the blackmailer."

"I'm sure you'll hear soon," I said. "Likely tonight." I had nothing to base that idea on. But she nodded as if I knew what I was talking about.

She handed me a piece of paper. "Here's the list from Pauline of who's coming to the sectional practice. And here's the choir list with the pictures. Shall we go through them?"

I'd decided we should try to come up with a shortlist of blackmailers. There were twenty-nine tenors in all. Only sixteen, including Anna and me, had said they would attend the sectional. So which of the fourteen had all of the means, motive and opportunity to commit the crime?

We crossed off two people right away: they hadn't attended the Tuesday-night practice. That left twelve who'd been there. Twelve who'd had the opportunity to lift the notebook from Anna's bag. Or did it?

I said, "The only time you left your bag unattended was when you came back from your phone call, put it on the floor and walked around talking to people. Right?"

"Right. I had the bag zipped up and under my arm the rest of the time."

"Then the only tenors who had an opportunity to take it would be people who were in the church for the last five minutes or so of the break. And these two"— I pointed to two headshots—"came back to the practice late from outside. They rushed in when the rest of the choir was seated and Richard was talking about the next song to practice. Do you remember?"

"Not really," Anna said.

"I do. I can see them so clearly. The ponytail man and the woman who wears zebra-stripe eyeglasses. There they are, in my memory, speed-walking to their spots at the end of the first tenor row.

Which is strange. I seem to have noticed them without knowing I'd noticed them."

"Maybe you have a videographic memory. The way some people have a photographic memory."

"Is that a thing?"

"It should be."

"Anyway, strike those two from the list."

We were down to ten. We cut two more who'd sat at the back of the church for the entire break and sold raffle tickets. That left eight.

Next, we looked at who had the means to commit the crime. But we couldn't eliminate anyone on that basis. Everyone had access to a computer and knowledge of how to set up and use an email account. We knew that since they'd all emailed Pauline to confirm their attendance at the sectional.

How about motive? The blackmailer was doing this for money, so who among our eight was broke?

"Not Carol," Anna said. She meant the woman I'd nicknamed Old Hippie. "She's a wealthy widow. I interviewed her for *Noontime* a few months ago about a huge donation she made to a hospital. A new wing is going up with her name on it."

I crossed her name off the list.

"Not Martin either," Anna said. Martin was the middle-aged man I called Tall Guy. He often came to practice in a suit, white shirt and tie. She said, "He's a high-priced corporate lawyer. Ten thousand dollars is what he'd spend on a weekend getaway."

"That's two down. Who's left that's poor? Or poor-ish?"

She made a face. "I hate talking about people like this."

"You'll get over it. Who else?"

"There's Brandon. He's been unemployed since he got his graduate degree, I think. Or is he working part-time at a coffee shop while he tries to find a job in his field? Whichever."

"What's his field?"

She had to think about that. "Could it be philosophy?"

"People with philosophy degrees don't actually expect to find jobs in their field, do they?"

"I don't know, but he told me last season he wasn't sure if he'd be back for this season. He couldn't afford it."

I circled his name on the list. "Yet he's back."

"Yes, he is." She looked down at the list. "Next is Pauline. She can't be the blackmailer. She's been in the choir for years, and she always hosts the tenor sectionals. And she has a good job, in insurance. So unless she's racked up some gambling debts or has a secret drug habit, I'd say she's out of the running."

"A secret drug habit? Her?"

"You're right. Cross her off." She kept going down the list. "I don't know anything about these two—Kristi and Carmen—

other than that they don't seem to like me much. What's their problem anyway?"

"They're just jealous of your looks and your success. But we can't dismiss them— Kristi has mentioned being short of money a few times. And those two are joined at the hip. They might even be working together. Mark them as maybes."

"Done."

"Now, what about the creepy guy with the tattoo on his neck?" The guy who'd probably won the Most Likely To Serve Hard Time Award in high school. If he'd even graduated. "What's his name again?" I found the photo of Sticky Fingers on the list. "Oscar. What's his story?"

"He collects a disability pension. He was injured on the job a few years ago. In a factory, I think."

"So he's not well-off."

"No. And frankly? I wouldn't be surprised if he had a criminal record."

"Do you think he could be in a biker gang? I heard someone refer to him as a biker once."

"He could. Though he seems nice enough. Friendly."

I said, "You have to watch out for the nice ones. Isn't that what they say?"

"Who says that?"

"Never mind. We've narrowed the list down to four people to watch at the practice: Kristi, Carmen, Brandon and Oscar." Especially Oscar. "Good for us."

Anna's phone made a clicking noise. "That's my incoming email signal. Maybe it's him!"

"Or her."

She picked up her phone, opened the email. She said, "It *is* him. Or her." And together, we read the message.

CHAPTER FOURTEEN

The email said:

You're smart to pay up. Now don't screw up. Follow these instructions and you'll have your precious journal back on Saturday.

1. Bring the $10,000 cash in $100 bills inside a sealed, unmarked 8 ½" by 11" manila envelope.

2. Get to the practice early enough that you can go to the main floor bathroom before the sectional starts.

3. Lift the radiator shelf in the bathroom, leave the envelope underneath it and replace the radiator shelf.

4. Do not return to the bathroom until after the practice is over. Don't be watching who goes in and out of there either.

5. After the practice, lift the shelf again and you'll find your journal there in an identical envelope.

6. Don't even think of trying to screw me around unless you want your smutty love life exposed to the world.

I said, "Your smutty love life?"

She sighed. "It's not *that* smutty. But I guess it's time I told you about it."

"Pretend I'm a doctor and the doctor-patient confidentiality rule applies."

Truth was, I didn't have to be any kind of smart to guess what Anna was hiding—she was having an affair with someone she shouldn't be. So I wasn't surprised when she confessed. She'd been sleeping with Tom Reynolds, the national news anchorman for her network, for the last year. Though he was fifty-three to her thirty-six. And married with three teenage children. Though he was a serious old-timey journalist. A guy who stood for ethics and integrity.

"There are no details about our sex life in the journal," she said. "Oh, I might have mentioned buying new lingerie or getting a Brazilian wax before meeting up with him, but there's nothing racier than that. The problem is that there's zero room for scandal in Tom's personal life. If he plays by the rules, he might last as the evening news anchor into his sixties. But if our affair is found out, that would be excuse enough for the network to replace him with someone younger and fresher. And maybe less white and male."

"Someone like you."

"Well, yes. Except it couldn't be me if I'm involved in the scandal."

"Then why are you risking everything by continuing to see each other? Why didn't this affair end before it started? Before the journal got stolen?"

"Because I'm irresistible?"

I hoped she was joking, but I was afraid she wasn't.

"Hey," I said, "don't let Kristi or Carmen hear you say anything like that. Talk about fuel for their fire."

"I was kidding."

Yeah right, she was.

"It sounds clichéd," she said, "but there's a real spark between Tom and me. I don't want him to leave his wife or kids. And I don't want to give up the connection we have either. It's too important to both of us. Too rare."

And too important to her career?

I said, "I get it. You need the journal back. Even if it means paying. Even if this payment is only the first of many."

"Yes. Though now that we have our shortlist of suspects...wait a second. Whoever wrote this email knows Pauline's house pretty well. Doesn't that mean we can rule out Kristi and Carmen? Since they're new to the choir this season?"

I had to think about that, review what I knew. "No," I said, after a minute. "We can't take them off the suspect list. They're friends with Pauline. She's the person who told them about the choir in the first place. The odds are good they've been inside her house before."

"Okay, fine. We still have four suspects to watch on Saturday. But can we expose the blackmailer *and* get the journal back?"

"We can try."

CHAPTER FIFTEEN

Our plan to unmask the blackmailer at the sectional depended on four things. One, Anna and I had to seem as if we weren't close. We couldn't arrive or leave together, or sit next to each other, or talk to each other much. My role was to watch the suspects and catch one of them in the act of switching the envelopes. I could do that best if the blackmailer didn't think that Anna had confided in her new best friend.

Two, I needed to be in a position where I could see who went into the bathroom.

Anna had explained that it was located off the front hall. The door to it could be seen from one end of the living room where Pauline held the practices, but not from the other. So I had to find and take a seat near the right end of the room.

Three, I had to remember to bring a big water bottle and drink from it throughout the practice. So I'd have an excuse to make frequent bathroom trips.

And four, the miniature spy camera hidden in the tissue box that Anna placed on top of the toilet tank had to work.

That's right. We put a miniature spy camera into play.

I thought of it as soon as I read the email about making the drop in the privacy of Pauline's bathroom. There was a gadget store in my mall. I went in there sometimes to look for gifts for Nathan. He was into gadgets. And the store had a section devoted to spy stuff.

The tissue-box spy camera cost over three hundred dollars, but the salesman at the store told me they had a two-week-trial policy on their more expensive items. So I bought one and kept the receipt. Anna's job was to set it up in the bathroom when she arrived at Pauline's house. At the same time as she placed her envelope full of cash under the radiator cover.

It might get awkward if Pauline went into the room during the practice and wondered where the new bathroom accessory had come from. But we figured hostesses don't have time to use the bathroom when they're entertaining. Or are distracted if they do.

Anna arrived twelve minutes before the sectional start time to do her drop and to set up the camera. I got to Pauline's house—a semi-detached two-story near the church—three minutes before one o'clock. Pregnant was on the front porch when I drove up.

And I could see Carmen and Tall Guy coming down the sidewalk half a block away.

The first few minutes after I walked into the house were hectic. There was a lot of *Hi, how are you?* going on, and *That looks delicious!* The last part being about the food we'd been instructed to bring. When I'd broken through the crowd and placed the lemon loaf I'd purchased on the dining table, I looked around for Anna. She was on the other side of the room, helping Pauline set up chairs. She didn't glance my way, but she gave the signal we'd agreed upon—she scratched her elbow. So far, so good.

I asked Pauline where the bathroom was, as if I didn't already know, and went inside. All was in order. The envelope of cash was still under the rad cover—I checked. The tissue box was on top of the toilet tank, pointing its secret camera at the rad, ready to be tripped by motion.

As per plan, Anna had placed a sweater on the chair that offered the best view of the bathroom door. When I sidled over there, she picked up the sweater and moved across the room to another seat.

I sat, tried to breathe slowly and took out my music binder. I counted heads without moving my lips. We were all present, sixteen of us, including the four suspects. I noted their positions. And that none of them looked nervous or sweaty.

The accompanist set up her keyboard, and the practice began.

The sectional was scheduled for two hours, with a fifteen-minute break in the middle. I didn't think the bathroom would get used much in the first hour, but I kept an eye on it anyway. By 1:50 PM, three people had visited it—two from our non-suspect list, and me. I'd decided in advance that it would look too obvious—and weird—if I went into the bathroom and checked the hiding spot after every single visitor. That's what the camera was for. But I couldn't resist checking that one time. I didn't need to—the money was still there.

When the break was announced, I stayed put. Smokers, including Oscar and Brandon, went outside. Hungry people swarmed the food table. Anna went to help Pauline in the kitchen, and—aha!—our suspect Carmen went to the bathroom. Followed by two other non-suspects. After the second, I took a big gulp of water from my bottle and took up a waiting position in the narrow hallway. When Old Hippie came out, I smiled at her, slipped inside and locked the door.

I waved at the tissue box, went straight for the rad cover and lifted it up. The envelope inside looked an awful lot like Anna's envelope. In fact, it *was* Anna's envelope, untouched, with the money still in it.

So Carmen was in the clear. I swore and replaced the rad cover. The blackmailer had to be Oscar, Brandon or Kristi. Unless our reasoning sucked, and it was someone else.

I flushed the toilet. I would not pee on camera, even if all the camera would film was my upper back. I washed and dried my hands, opened the door and came face-to-face with Brandon standing in the hall, his man-purse slung over his shoulder. As usual, he smelled like cigarettes.

"Hey," he said and stepped past me, went inside, closed the door.

I pulled my phone out of my pocket. It was 2:08 PM. I walked backward to my chair, sat down, and without taking my eyes off the bathroom door, wrote the time on the edge of my sheet music. And waited.

At the dining table, Pauline said to Green Hair, "So it seems there's a pickpocket in the choir, have you heard?"

I pricked up my ears but kept my eyes focused on the bathroom door.

Green Hair said, "No! Really? Someone's stealing?"

"Apparently. Several people noticed small amounts of cash missing from their wallets after practice. Ten dollars here, twenty there. No credit cards, just bills. No one thought much of it until word got out several people had misplaced money."

"Hey, that happened to me," Pregnant said. "I was twenty dollars short one night but I thought I must have spent it. Are you telling me someone in the choir stole it?"

"Crooks are everywhere," Oscar said. Because it took one to know one?

"That's awful," Green Hair said. "Who would do that?"

"Someone desperate," Pauline said.

I set back my mental DVD to break time at the first choir practice I'd attended, and saw it all. Kristi and Carmen leaving their pew to go sign up for the solo auditions. Me, standing up, looking around the church. Anna in the corner, writing in her journal. Brandon moving around in the pew behind me. Acting awkward when I spoke to him. Right after he must have helped himself to money from Pregnant's purse.

Or had Kristi stolen it? She'd had access too. So had Oscar.

By the time Brandon came out of the bathroom at 2:13 PM, the practice had resumed. He didn't look guilty when he returned to his seat. Or no more than usual. But it killed me to wait the ten minutes I thought were long enough to make my next visit to the bathroom look innocent.

After nine minutes, I muttered, "I've drunk too much water today," ran down to the bathroom, nipped inside. I locked the door, put down my bag, held my breath and lifted the rad cover.

The switch had been made.

CHAPTER SIXTEEN

I removed the notebook from the envelope, flipped it open, and made sure it was Anna's original one. Sure enough, I found her last entry, the word *SPICIER*. I placed the notebook in my bag. We'd agreed beforehand that whoever got to it first should take it for safekeeping. I stuffed the tissue-box camera in my bag too.

When I came out, I had a sudden fear that Brandon might have left while I was inside, and taken the money with him. But he was in his chair, singing "Sunny Days." I'd sunny day him. I pulled a hair clip out of my bag and put my hair up—my signal to Anna that I had the notebook. Smooth operator that she was, she had no reaction other than to scratch her elbow again.

I joined in singing, and somehow got through the next forty minutes. As soon as the practice ended, I jumped up from my chair and waylaid Brandon. "Can I talk to you privately?" I said. "Outside. You can smoke."

The panicked look in his eyes told me he knew he was nailed. But his voice was calm. "Sure," he said. He stood up, pulled a pack of cigarettes out of his bag and held it out to me. "Want one?"

I said no thanks and led him out to Pauline's back garden. I picked a spot to stand in that was a good twelve feet away from the door, next to some bushes. I took a deep breath and used my manager voice. Like he was a shoplifter I'd caught in my store.

"I know what you did. So unless you want to be reported to the police, arrested and charged with extortion, I suggest you give me back the cash. Right now."

He didn't say anything for maybe thirty seconds. He just stood and took a drag on his cigarette, and looked past my head at the yard next door.

"Hello?" I said.

"What's it to you anyway?"

"What?"

"Are you Anna's agent or something? Her manager? Her personal assistant?"

"I'm her friend. Are you going to give me back the cash or not?"

"How do I know you're not going to run off with it?"

"She's waiting for me down the street."

"So you say."

"You want me to get her back here?" I pulled out my phone. "I'll text her right now and tell her you want to talk to her. Explain why you blackmailed her."

"Fuck it." He reached inside his bag, pulled out the envelope, handed it over. "Here. Happy now?"

My hands were shaking a little. I opened it, checked inside. It looked like the cash was all there. "Yes, I am. Thank you." I tucked the envelope into my bag. "So, why *did* you do it?"

He exhaled a long plume of smoke. "Because I'm broke. I got laid off from my shit job and I can't make my rent and I don't want to move back in with my parents. Not after they supported me all through graduate school. I knew Anna was making big bucks on television. I figured she could afford to spread some wealth around."

"This is how you justify blackmailing someone who's been nice to you?"

"Look. I thought I could make some quick cash easily if I wasn't too greedy. If I didn't ask for too much. I gambled and lost, that's all." He dropped his cigarette on the ground and stepped on it. "What's crazy is that I didn't even steal the goddamned journal. I found it in my bag when I got home from practice that night. Anna must have slipped it in there by mistake when she was sitting next to me. We both had black canvas bags on the floor and they look pretty much the same."

"Come on."

"I'm telling the truth. All that ruckus at practice about a missing notebook. Then I get home, unpack my bag, and there it is. After she'd said how important it was, I had to read it." He pulled out another cigarette and lit it. "It took me a while to see why she cared so much. Most of the entries were boring as shit. When I finally came to the part about her affair with that anchorman, I was disappointed. I thought there'd be something juicier. Like racist rants or kinky sex stories. Though there was enough dirt to make her pay up."

I looked at his shifty eyes and down-turned mouth. So this was where his higher education had taken him. "You'll quit the choir now, of course."

"Do I have to?"

"I think so. Unless you want me to report you for stealing cash from women's purses at practice."

"Christ, you caught me doing that too?"

"Yes, I did."

He shook his head. "You can hardly blame me for helping myself when all those women left their bags around, open. The cash was practically falling out of their wallets. And they could spare twenty or forty bucks, all of them. That's what they spend on coffee in a week. But how'd you know I was the culprit? What are you, an undercover cop? A criminology major?"

"I have a videographic memory."

"A what?"

"I saw you lifting money from a purse once. And I'm not a cop. I'm the manager of a retail store."

"Yeah?" He looked me in the eye for the first time. "Which one? I could use a new shit job. Any chance you're hiring?"

CHAPTER SEVENTEEN

After I told Brandon I wouldn't hire him, no way, I left Pauline's and walked to the car. I really was supposed to meet Anna down the street, but I took a roundabout route to get there. And on the way, I pulled over, opened the journal and skimmed it.

Like you wouldn't have?

I had to agree with Brandon. Most of the thoughts and ideas Anna had recorded in the notebook were dull. And the details she'd written down about her private meetings with Tom Reynolds were more embarrassing than dirty. I won't quote her.

I'll just say that she had pet names for some of his body parts. And for hers. And the words *big* and *little* might have been parts of those pet names.

Whatever. The most damaging information in the journal was not what Anna had written about the affair. It was that the journal provided proof of it. Proof that was worthless to Brandon, now that I could turn him in for attempted blackmail and theft anytime.

But could knowledge of the affair be worth something to me?

I put that question aside to ponder later, and drove off to meet Anna. I handed over the journal and the cash, and gave her a brief report on my talk with Brandon. She hugged me, and cried a little, and said I was a genius. I wasn't, but it was good of her to say.

"I want to take you out for a nice dinner," she said. "To thank you."

I said sure, let's do that, and we made a date to have dinner at Sterling the following Tuesday, before choir practice.

On the Monday, I returned the tissue-box camera as defective—it hadn't taped a thing, stupid machine. And I told Joanne and Nathan an edited version of how *The Mystery of the Missing Notebook* had gone down. I said that this sketchy guy Brandon had picked it up by mistake and I'd figured that out. And Anna was taking me out to dinner to thank me for my help.

"That's generous of her," Joanne said and started to sing "I Gotta Feeling." The line about how good my night was going to be. I cut her off. "It's a dinner out, that's all. No big deal."

"Maybe Anna could shoot a segment of her show at Sterling," Nathan said. "The angle could be our new menu that features local ingredients and wines. Can you find a way to suggest it to her?" Oh, Nathan.

On the night of the thank-you dinner, Nathan came by our table. He looked good in his work clothes: black dress pants, black shirt, skinny silver tie. He kissed me hello on the cheek, introduced himself to Anna and presented us with glasses of champagne. On the house.

Anna said, "Why, thank you! And champagne is perfect for the occasion, because I heard some more good news today. *Noontime* has been picked up for national distribution! Isn't that exciting? In fact, we've got so much to celebrate—let's order a bottle of champagne. Can you arrange that, Nathan?"

He said he'd be happy to, and I could almost see the dollar signs in his eyes when he walked away.

Anna said, "He's cute. And I can tell he really likes you."

"He's a solid guy. Sweet. And supportive. When I had to film that video audition for work? He did the shooting and the editing and everything. He did an ace job too."

"I'd love to see your video sometime."

"Really? Because I uploaded it to my Facebook profile. I could show it to you right now."

"Oh yes, show me," she said. And if she was faking interest, she faked it well.

I accessed Facebook on my phone and played it for her. The first minute of it anyway. I didn't want to bore her with the whole thing.

"You look wonderful!" she said. "That outfit is so flattering. And the makeup. You sound good too, from what I can hear. Send me the link, will you? So I can see the rest?"

"Thanks, I will." I put down my phone, picked up the menu. Looked at it like I hadn't already decided what to have. "So, *Noontime* is going national, huh? You must be happy."

"So happy." Quietly, she said, "What with that news and getting the journal back,

I've had a fantastic week. And when I think about how depressed I was last Wednesday at this time! What a difference a few days make." She lifted her glass. "To friends who come through in a crunch."

I clinked glasses with her and sipped the champagne.

"Everything on the menu sounds delicious," she said. "I'm trying to decide between the duck and the scallops for the main course. What do you think?"

We talked about the menu. The waiter came over with a bottle of champagne in an ice bucket. We finished our first glasses and watched him open it. He poured us each a second glass. We ordered our food. And during all that, I thought about the gap between Anna and me. About how we must look sitting together at the table—the TV star and the nobody. About how with my lack of education and experience, I had little chance of making it to even her level of fame and success. Unless, of course, I decided to do a little blackmailing of my own.

Think about it. I had the means—I knew about the affair. I had a motive: not money, but the desire for a new job, a new future. In television, working with her, on the national version of *Noontime*. And when it came to opportunity, I could speak up right there, at the dinner table.

I could tell her I had some ideas for how to "spice" up the show. Like that a funny bit might be to ask people what nicknames they give their own and their sweetheart's privates. Wouldn't that make for a laugh? And while my meaning sank in and the color drained from her face, I could mention I'd always wanted to work in TV. Hell, I could be as bold as Brandon and ask her right out if she was hiring. I'd leave it unsaid that she would know what to do if she didn't want her secrets made public.

I took my first sip of champagne from the second glass. Anna was well into hers, and was going on about her plans for the show. She wanted to work in more food segments. Travel to small towns and find hidden gem bakeries. Visit wineries. Conduct cook-offs for regional food specialties. Have the winners of the cook-offs come on the show and cook with her. "What do you think? Would those ideas attract more viewers your age?"

Before I could answer, the waiter brought our first course. We were sharing the chef's signature dish, a salad made with seven kinds of exotic vegetables. It came piled six inches high on the plate and was crowned with deep-fried taro root.

"Look at those colors! That presentation! It's beautiful!" Anna said. "I should take a picture for my blog. Do you mind waiting a second before we eat it?"

"Not at all. Go to town." I leaned back so no part of my body would be in the picture. And watched her take pictures from this angle and that.

I couldn't blackmail her for a job. Any more than I could have taken the money from the wallet I found in the mall parking lot that time. I couldn't lift cash from Joanne's purse. Or steal merchandise from the store. Or date someone who already had a wife or a girlfriend. To do those things would be dishonest, and wrong. If that's what you had to do to get ahead, I wasn't going anywhere.

Anna finished taking her pictures. "All done," she said. "Dig in. And what do you think about my ideas for the show?"

I poked my fork into the tower of salad and pulled out a pea shoot. "If you really want to appeal to young people, I think you should go bigger and smaller at the same time. Try to find the best cheap hangover brunches. The best restaurant meals for less than ten dollars. Get chefs to give recipes for gourmet dishes that can be cooked on one stove burner with less than five ingredients.

Or not cooked at all." I pointed to the salad. "You'd want to talk about food that's the opposite of this. Because let's face it: people like me can't afford to eat food like this unless someone like you is paying."

She was chewing, but she held one finger up in the waiting signal and opened her eyes wide. When she'd swallowed, she said, "That is such a good idea, Steph. Or such a bunch of good ideas." She put down her fork, opened her bag and took out a black notebook and a pen. "Let me write those down."

"You're still using those notebooks for your journal?"

"No, I learned my lesson. From now on, the notebook I carry around with me will contain work notes, and nothing else. I keep my personal journal at home, locked up."

"Good idea."

"And I want you to know that I've stopped seeing the person I was seeing. For now. We're taking a break. A break that could become permanent."

"What person was that?" I said. Ha-ha. I was so discreet.

She made her notes and closed the notebook.

"Listen," she said. "We haven't known each other very long, but I have excellent people instincts. And now that we worked together so well sorting out my little problem, I want to ask you something.

"I don't know how to ask it without sounding like I think I'm a big shot. And I don't want to talk down to you either. So I'll just say it." She cleared her throat. "Is there a chance you'd want to come work for me at *Noontime*? As an assistant producer? The salary would be low to start.

But I think that someone as bright and personable and attractive as you could go places. In time. If everything goes right."

I stared at her. Was I hearing things? Or had I just been offered a half-decent job? A real opportunity. And without having to blackmail her to get it.

She said, "I don't mean to suggest that you're not going places now, at your present job. The places I'm talking about going are just different places."

"I'm interested," I said. "For sure." Pay cut or no pay cut. I had some money in the bank. And I hadn't worn out my welcome with Joanne, not yet.

"Wonderful!" she said.

Nathan came over just then and asked how we were doing. "Everything's lovely, thanks," Anna said and gave him a dazzling smile.

I smiled big too.

KIM MORITSUGU is the author of four previous novels. *The Glenwood Treasure* (2003) was shortlisted for the Arthur Ellis Award for Best Crime Novel. She also leads a walking tour for Heritage Toronto, teaches creative writing at the Humber School for Writers, writes a food blog called *The Hungry Novelist* and sings in a community rock/pop choir.

* * *

I was a little drunk by the time we got to choir practice. Who wouldn't be after five glasses of champagne? So it was the alcohol talking—or singing—when I blasted out the tenor part at top volume during "I'm So Excited," the first song we sang that night.

Joanne told me later she could barely hear Carmen, the soloist, over the noise coming from my corner of the tenor section. "If I didn't know better," she said, "I'd think you're really into the choir now. Like I hoped you would be."

I said the choir was all right. Okay, more than all right. But that the reason I'd gotten carried away was that I was tipsy. And pumped about the offer Anna had made me over dinner.

"What offer?" Joanne said.

Finally, I had a good story to tell.